W9-BUM-416

SCOOBY-DOO! AND THE HOWLING WOLFMAN

Written by
James Gelsey

For Toby and Seth

visit us at www.abdopublishing.com

Reinforced library bound edition published in 2013 by Spotlight, a division of the ABDO Group, PO Box 398166, Minneapolis, MN 55439. Spotlight produces high-quality reinforced library bound editions for schools and libraries. Published by agreement with Warner Bros.-A Time Warner Company.

Printed in the United States of America, North Mankato, Minnesota.

102012

012013

♻ This book contains at least 10% recycled materials.

No part of this publication may be reproduced in whole or in part, or stored in a retrieval system, or transmitted in any form or by any means, electronic, mechanical, photocopying, recording, or otherwise, without written permission of the publisher.

Copyright © 2012 Hanna-Barbera.
SCOOBY-DOO and all related characters and elements are trademarks of and © Hanna-Barbera.
WB Shield: ™ & © Warner Bros. Entertainment Inc.
(s12)

Cover and interior illustrations by Duendes Del Sur.

Cataloging-in-Publication Data

Gelsey, James.
Scooby-Doo! and the howling wolfman / written by James Gelsey.
p. cm. -- (Scooby-Doo Mysteries)
[1. Scooby-Doo (Fictitious character)--Fiction. 2. Dogs--Fiction. 3. Mystery and detective stories.]

ISBN 978-1-61479-046-4 (reinforced library bound edition)

All Spotlight books are reinforced library bindings and manufactured in the United States of America.

"Yee-haw!" Shaggy called from the back of the Mystery Machine. Suddenly, a giant lasso flew to the front and landed around Velma. She dropped the book she was reading.

"Hey, you guys!" Fred yelled back. "Be careful with that thing. You lassoed Velma!"

Shaggy and Scooby-Doo came to the front of the van. They were both wearing cowboy hats.

"Like, sorry, Velma," Shaggy said.

"Reah." Scooby nodded. "Rorry, Relma."

Velma lifted the rope over her head.

"What are you two doing with this lasso anyway?"

"Just getting ready for the ranch," Shaggy answered.

Scooby jumped onto Shaggy's back. "Ride 'em, rowboy!" Scooby barked happily. Everyone laughed as Fred steered the van through a wooden gate.

"Hey, everybody," Daphne said. "Look at that!" She pointed to a statue of a giant wolf standing just inside the gate. It had a fierce gaze and big, sharp teeth.

"That's where the Lone Wolf Ranch got its name," Velma read from her guidebook. "This area was full of wolves when the ranch was founded a hundred years ago."

"There's a legend they used to tell around the campfire when I came here as a kid," Fred said. "During a full moon one night a hundred years ago, a giant wolf appeared and drove all the other wolves away. So the owners made a statue of the giant wolf to protect them for all time."

"Some people believe the giant wolf was really a wolfman," Velma added. "And that his spirit is still trapped inside the statue to keep the ranch safe."

"Like, it sounds kinda creepy to me," Shaggy said.

"Believe me," Fred said, "there's nothing creepy about this place."

"Then what's that?" Daphne asked as she pointed out the window.

Fred stopped the van short as a scary-looking man stepped in front of them. He had a craggy face and wild hair sticking out in all directions. He carried what looked like a big hammer.

"Rikes!" Scooby cried. He and Shaggy jumped under the seat.

The man glared through the windshield with fierce gray eyes.

"There's a full moon tonight," the man warned. "Leave now, before the wolfman comes and gets you all." He walked slowly backward up the road, never taking his eyes off the gang. Then he quickly turned and ran off into the woods.

"Jinkies," Velma said. "Who was that?"

"I don't recognize him," Fred replied.

"Is he g-g-gone?" Shaggy whispered from under the seat.

"You can come out now," Daphne said.

"Like, it's not too late to turn the van around, is it?" Shaggy asked. "Scooby-Doo and I just remembered we have to be someplace very important."

"Where's that?" Daphne asked.

"Anyplace where there's no wolfman!" Shaggy answered.

Fred started driving the van again. "Don't let that crazy man bother you," he said.

"Like, too late," Shaggy replied.

"If we leave now," Daphne said, "you'll miss the big barbecue."

"And the campfire," Velma added, "where you can roast marsh-mallows."

"Rarshrallows?" Scooby asked with a big smile.

Shaggy and Scooby looked at each other. They huddled together and whispered back and forth.

"Scooby and I have decided to stay," Shaggy said.

"What made you change your mind?" Velma asked.

"Wolfman," Scooby said.

Fred, Daphne, and Velma all looked puzzled.

"Like, if he's really coming back tonight after a hundred years," Shaggy explained, "he's going to be hungry. He'll be so busy gobbling up all that food, he won't have time to gobble us up!"

Everyone laughed as Fred steered the Mystery Machine into the ranch's parking area.

Chapter 2

The gang got out of the van and looked around. Across from the parking area stood a big red barn. The barn was next to a big open space surrounded by a low wooden fence. Two horses were running around inside the corral, and a lone bull stood next to the fence. On the other side of the corral, there was a log-cabin-style bunkhouse.

"Howdy, partners," someone said. The gang turned and saw two men standing there. They were both dressed in cowboy outfits and wore big cowboy hats. They looked so much alike it was hard to tell them apart.

"Hello, Fred," the man on the left said. "You've sure grown since we saw you last!"

"Put 'er there, partner," the other man said. He reached over and slapped Fred on the back. "Thanks for coming for the big celebration."

"Hi, Flint. Hi, Colt," Fred said. "Thanks for inviting me and my friends."

"Any friends of yours are friends of ours," Colt said. "Has Fred told you all about his summers here as a kid? Boy, he and Bucky

Tanner sure used to get into some trouble."

Fred blushed a little. He turned to the gang.

"Everyone, I'd like you to meet Colt and Flint Hopster," Fred said. "They own the Lone Wolf Ranch. In fact, their great-great-grandfather founded the ranch a hundred years ago."

Fred turned to introduce his friends. "This is Daphne, Velma, Shaggy, and Scooby-Doo," Fred said.

The man on the left took off his hat. He had short black hair. "Nice to meet you," he said. "I'm Flint."

"And I'm Colt," the other man said, taking off his hat. He had long, sandy-colored hair pulled back in a ponytail.

"I was just about to tell everyone that the whole ranch is just like I remembered," Fred said with a big smile.

Colt looked right at Flint.

"What did I tell you?" Colt said. "We shouldn't change a thing."

"You're wrong!" Flint said. "We've got to expand this place if we want to save it. And if you won't do anything, I will!" Flint stomped away angrily.

Colt looked at the gang and put his hat back on.

"Sorry about that," he said. "The ranch is in a little trouble, and we can't seem to agree on what to do. I convinced Flint to hold this big hundredth-birthday celebration to drum up business. If it fails, I don't know what we'll do. I just hope Flint doesn't sell the horseshoes."

"What's so special about horseshoes?" Velma asked.

Colt smiled. "That must have sounded funny, all right," he said. "Our great-great-grandfather made four gold horseshoes when he opened the ranch. We're going to be showing them tonight as part of the celebration. They're worth a lot of money now, but I think our great-great-grandfather really meant them to be good-luck charms."

"Along with the wolf statue," Fred said.

"I see you still remember Coyote Cal's campfire stories," Colt said. "Anyway, Flint keeps talking about selling the horseshoes so we can make the ranch a big cowboy resort. I'd rather keep it small and friendly. Like the way you remember it, Fred. I think it's what our great-great-grandfather would want."

"I can tell you what I want," Shaggy whispered to Scooby. "A great big burger."

"Reah, reah." Scooby nodded. His big pink tongue swept across his lips.

"Speaking of burgers," Colt said, "why don't you go on over and say hello to Gabby."

"You mean Gabby Tanner's still the cook?" Fred asked.

"Yup," Colt answered. "And Bucky's still here, too. He helps out, does odd jobs and such."

"Thanks, Colt," Fred said. "We'll see you later. Come on, gang, it's time to meet one of the best cooks in the world." Fred started walking toward the bunkhouse, and everyone followed.

As the gang passed the corral, Shaggy and Scooby stopped for a look. Daphne turned and saw them stop.

"Let's go, you two," she called.

"We'll be right there," Shaggy said. "We just want to watch some real cowboys in action."

"All right, but stay out of trouble," Daphne said. She turned and continued walking.

"Like, don't worry, Daph," Shaggy said. "What kind of trouble could we possibly get into?"

Chapter 3

Shaggy and Scooby stopped next to the wooden fence. They could see two horses running around inside the corral. They saw a cowboy climb up and stand on top of one of the fence posts. He twirled a big lasso over his head and then threw it into the corral. It landed on one of the horses.

"Didja see that, Scoob?" Shaggy asked. "Catching a moving horse is a lot harder than lassoing a sitting Velma."

"Roh, reah?" Scooby said. "Watch ris!" He grabbed a rope lying on the ground and stood up on a post. There was still one horse running around the corral. Scooby twirled the lasso over his head and threw it into the corral. It sailed through the air and landed on something.

"Way to go, Scooby-Doo!" Shaggy called. "You're a real cowdog!"

Scooby got off the post and pulled the rope in. But instead of seeing the horse, he was face-to-face with an angry bull.

"Snort!" the bull growled at Scooby through the fence. The bull lowered his head

and scratched the ground with his front hoof.

"Zoinks!" Shaggy yelled. "Look out, Scoob, he's going to charge!"

Just as the bull was about to charge at Scooby, a big man stepped in front of it. He stared right into the bull's angry eyes. The bull stopped snorting and then ran away.

The man turned around and looked right at Scooby and Shaggy. He had gray eyes and was holding a hammer.

"Rikes!" Scooby yelled, jumping into Shaggy's arms.

"Like, it's the creepy man from the road!" Shaggy called. They turned and ran toward the bunkhouse.

At the bunkhouse, Fred, Daphne, and Velma were on the front porch talking to an old woman and a young man.

"It is sure nice to see you again, Bucky," Fred said to the young man. "And you, too, Gabby. I've really missed your cooking."

"That's mighty nice of you to say, Freddie," the woman said. She was a short woman with streaks of gray in her black hair. She wore a big denim apron over her clothes. It was stained with all kinds of food.

"Who're these folks?" Bucky asked.

"This is Daphne and Velma," Fred said. "Shaggy and Scooby are around here somewhere."

"Make way!" Shaggy called as he and Scooby ran toward the bunkhouse. They ran onto the porch and hid behind the others.

"What's up with you two?" Velma asked.

Scooby's tail peeked out from behind Daphne. It pointed at the man walking toward the porch.

"That's just Coyote Cal," Bucky said. "He's a hired hand on the ranch Been here for years."

"That's Coyote Cal?" Fred asked. "He looks a lot different from when I was here."

"That's because he was bitten by a wolf-man," Bucky joked.

"That's enough, Bucky," Gabby said.

Coyote Cal slowly walked up to the bunkhouse porch. The big hammer was hanging through a loop on his dungarees. He took a red handkerchief from the pocket of his denim shirt and wiped his forehead. He never took his eyes off the gang.

"I warned you kids not to come here," he said. "Strangers aren't welcome here. Not tonight."

"Now, Cal," Gabby said. "Don't you recognize this boy? It's Fred, Bucky's old friend from way back. They used to play together during the summer."

Cal squinted and stared at Fred.

"I guess he's okay, if you say so," Cal said. "But there's still no reason for all these people to be around tonight with what's been going on around here."

"You mean getting ready for the party?" Daphne asked.

"He means getting ready to see the gold horseshoes," Bucky said.

"Of course he means the party," Gabby said. "I've been preparing the food for days."

"I don't mean the party," Cal said. "I mean all the howling we've been hearing the past few nights."

"Cal thinks the curse of the Lone Wolf will come true tonight," Bucky said. He looked at Shaggy and Scooby with an evil grin. "When the full moon rises, the moonbeams will shatter the statue of the Lone Wolf and release his spirit into the night. The wolfman will return! Aaaa-ooooooooh!"

Shaggy and Scooby dove behind Daphne again. Bucky laughed.

"Now, Bucky," Gabby scolded him.

"Don't laugh, Bucky," Cal said. "As sure as we're standing here, that wolfman is coming tonight with the full moon. Don't say I didn't warn you." Cal turned and walked away.

"Don't pay any attention to Cal," Gabby said. "He's just angry that he's still a ranch hand. He keeps giving Colt and Flint all kinds of crazy advice on how to run and save the ranch. But they won't listen to him. Or his crazy ideas about the curse of the howling wolfman."

"Speaking of curses," Shaggy said, "Scooby and I have our own curse."

"What curse is that?" Velma asked.

"Like, the curse of the growling stomach," Shaggy replied. "We're hungry."

"Well, come on in and have a slice of my famous peach cobbler," Gabby said. "It'll hold you over until the big barbecue tonight. And you don't have to wait for a full moon to eat it!" Everyone laughed as they followed Gabby and Bucky inside the bunkhouse.

Chapter 4

That night, everyone on the Lone Wolf Ranch gathered in the corral for the big celebration. A small wooden stage stood at one end of the corral. A long table full of food was set up at the other end. The gang came out of the bunkhouse all dressed up in cowboy outfits. Shaggy and Scooby wore their big cowboy hats.

"Hey, Scooby-Doo," Shaggy said. "It's time for a real buckaroo barbecue, so let's mosey on over, partner."

Shaggy and Scooby led the way to the corral. The food table was set with the largest

25

selection of barbecue food they had ever seen. There was barbecue chicken, barbecue ribs, barbecue beef, barbecue beans, barbecue corn, barbecue potatoes, barbecue carrots, barbecue hamburgers, barbecue hot dogs, and even barbecue pizza!

Gabby and Bucky were busy behind the table. She filled empty platters and helped serve the food.

The gang grabbed some plates.

"Everything looks and smells great, Gabby," Fred said. "This sure brings back memories."

"Hey, Fred," Bucky said, "remember the time Mom baked a dozen blackberry pies? We took them back to our secret hideout and ate every last one."

"We had stomachaches for days," Fred laughed. "But it was worth it!"

26

Colt and Flint walked over to the table. Flint was holding a small metal box under his arm. He grabbed a piece of chicken while Colt looked up at the sky.

"It's a full moon," Colt said.

"Would you forget about the curse?" Flint said. "I told you, Cal's crazy. I still don't understand why you want to keep him."

"He knows more about this place than anyone," Colt said. "I can't fire him."

"Well, you know we won't be able to afford to keep the whole staff much longer," Flint said. "So start thinking about who you *can* fire. Now let's get this thing started." Flint walked away before Colt could respond. Colt turned to the gang.

"Looks like we'll be starting soon," Colt

said. "Come up front for a good view." Colt left and followed Flint over to the stage.

"Bucky, you'd better get some pies from the kitchen," Gabby said. "I want to be ready to serve dessert right after Flint and Colt finish." Bucky nodded and walked out of the corral.

"Ladies and gentlemen, cowboys and cowgirls," Colt announced from the stage. "May I have your attention please?" Everyone in the crowd walked toward the platform. The gang made their way to the front. They

could see Flint standing next to Colt. Flint was still holding the small metal box.

"Most of you know the story of Lone Wolf Ranch," Colt said. "Our great-great-grandfather found gold on this land. He sold most of the gold and used what was left to make four golden horseshoes. These horseshoes have been in our family for one hundred years. Tonight, it is our pleasure to-—"

"Aaaaa-oooooooooooooooooooooh!"

A loud howl suddenly filled the air. Everyone was silent.

"That does it!" Flint said. "I'm going to take care of Cal once and for all!" Flint gave Colt the metal box. He ran off the platform and into the woods.

"Stay calm, everybody," Colt said. "Just someone's idea of a little joke. No reason to be alarmed."

"AAAA-OOOOOOOOOOOOOOOH!" The howl was louder. Just then something ran out of the woods and onto the platform.

"It's a wolf!" Daphne cried.

"Jinkies!" Velma yelled. "It's not a wolf. It's a wolfman!"

"Wolfman!" shouted Shaggy and Scooby as they ran away through the crowd.

The wolfman snarled and growled at the crowd. Everyone gasped. Colt was so surprised he couldn't move. The wolfman turned and pushed Colt down. He grabbed the metal box. He howled at the full moon and then ran off into the woods.

A moment later, Flint ran onto the stage. He was out of breath. He helped Colt get up.

"The statue of the Lone Wolf has been smashed," Flint said. The crowd gasped.

"I warned you people about the curse!" Coyote Cal yelled. He was standing on one of the fence posts around the corral. "If you had listened to me, none of this would have happened. Now the ranch will pay!" He turned and disappeared into the woods. The crowd quickly scattered as everyone ran toward their bunks.

"The horseshoes are gone," Flint said.

"How do you know?" Fred asked.

"Because they were in that metal box," Flint said. "We were going to show them as part of the celebration."

"The ranch is doomed for sure," Colt said. "What are we going to do now?"

Fred, Daphne, and Velma nodded at one another. "Don't worry, we're on the case!" they said.

31

Chapter 5

The next morning, the gang met by the corral.

"Okay, everyone, let's start by splitting up," Fred said. "Daphne and I will look around here and down by the Lone Wolf statue."

"I'll follow the wolf's tracks into the woods," Velma said. "They may lead us to some clues."

"Scooby and I will look for clues around the kitchen," Shaggy said. "The wolfman might have built up an appetite."

"Oh, no you don't, you two," Velma said.

"You're coming with me. There's a lot of ground to cover out there, and I'll need all the help I can get."

Velma walked across the corral, keeping her eyes on the dusty ground. She was looking for wolf prints.

"There!" Velma said, pointing at the ground. "Follow those prints!"

Velma, Shaggy, and Scooby followed the trail of wolf prints into the woods. They walked around rocks and under branches.

"Man, four helpings of cowboy breakfast must not have been enough," Shaggy said. "I'm getting pooped." He was starting to breathe heavily. Even Scooby was panting.

"That's because we're walking uphill," Velma said. "Remember to watch where you're going. There are a lot of things to trip on in these woods."

"A lot of things to what?" Shaggy asked.

"To trip——" Velma began. "Oooops!" Velma suddenly fell over a small rock. Her eyeglasses flew off her face as she landed in a pile of soft moss.

"Relma!" Scooby exclaimed. He ran over to her.

"Jinkies," Velma said, sitting up. "I guess I didn't see that rock. Now we have to find my glasses. I can't see a thing without them."

"Not to worry, Velma," Shaggy said. "Scooby and I will find them in a flash. C'mon, Scoob."

Shaggy and Scooby started searching for Velma's glasses. Velma crawled around on her hands and knees, patting the ground around her. She crawled a few more feet and reached out her hand. This time she patted a furry foot.

"Scooby, don't just stand there," Velma said. "Help me up." Velma reached out and felt a furry paw take her hand. "I'll give you two Scooby Snacks if you find my glasses first, Scooby."

34

"Hey, Velma, Scooby and I found your glasses," Shaggy called. He and Scooby walked up to Velma and handed her the glasses.

Velma was puzzled. "If Scooby's with you, Shaggy," she said, "then who just helped me up?"

Velma, Shaggy, and Scooby all turned and looked behind them. It was the wolfman!

"Wolfman!" they shouted as they all turned and ran away.

The wolfman let out a big growl. "GRRRRRRRRR!"

Velma jumped behind a big bush to hide. The wolfman swiped his paw at Shaggy and Scooby. They turned and ran into the woods.

"Faster, Scoob!" Shaggy said, trying to push Scooby along. "He's gaining on us!" Shaggy and Scooby ran as fast as they could. They weaved in and out of trees. They jumped over rocks and ducked under branches. The wolfman stayed close behind, growling all the way.

"This way, Scooby," Shaggy said. He and Scooby made a sudden turn and ran toward a clearing.

"I think we lost him, Scooby," Shaggy said. "But we'd better hide somewhere, just in case." As they ran, they looked for a place to hide. Scooby then saw a big hollow log lying on the ground.

"Raggy! Rin rere!" Scooby barked, dashing into the log. Shaggy quickly followed.

"He'll never find us in here," Shaggy said. It was cramped inside the log. Shaggy and Scooby had to lie perfectly straight. "Now I know what a sardine must feel like."

They heard a rustling sound in the bushes. Someone was walking toward them. Before Shaggy could stop him, Scooby poked his head out one end of the log.

"Relma?" Scooby barked.

"Grrrrrrrrrowl!" It was the wolfman.

Scooby pulled his head back in just as the wolfman swiped at the log.

"Nice going, Scoob," Shaggy said. "Now he's going to get us for sure!"

The log started to rock.

"Hey, what's going on?" Shaggy asked.

With a great roar, the wolfman gave the log a big push. It slowly rolled over a rock. Then it started picking up speed and rolled all the way down the hill. They were heading right for the ranch.

"Aaaaaa-ooooooooooh!" howled the wolf-man from on top of the hill.

"Heeeelllpppp!" yelled Shaggy and Scooby from inside the log.

Chapter 6

Fred and Daphne were walking toward the bunkhouse when they heard a rumbling coming from the woods.

"Relp! Relp!"

"That sounds like Scooby!" Daphne exclaimed.

They looked up and saw the log rolling down the hill. It rolled under the wooden fence and stopped right in the middle of the corral.

"They must be in there! Come on, Daphne," Fred said. They ran over to the log.

"Shaggy? Scooby? Are you all right?" Daphne asked.

Shaggy and Scooby slowly crawled out of the log.

"Man, now I know what my clothes feel like in the dryer," Shaggy said. "Are you okay, Scoob?"

"I rink ro," Scooby said. Scooby stood up and started walking. But instead of going straight, he walked in circles. He was dizzy from the ride in the log.

"What happened to you two?" Fred asked. "And where's Velma?"

"Right here," Velma said behind them. Everyone turned.

"Relma!" Scooby exclaimed. He staggered over to give her a big hug. But because he was still dizzy, he walked right past her and hugged a fence post instead.

"Like, we thought the wolfman got you," Shaggy said.

"I was hiding behind some bushes, so he never found me," Velma said. "On my way back here to get help, I spotted the wolfman's tracks again. So I followed them and found a clue." She held out a piece of torn denim cloth.

"Zoinks! Like, that looks like the kind of shirt the wolfman was wearing," Shaggy said.

"But the most interesting thing is where I found this piece of cloth," Velma said.

"Where?" Fred asked.

"The tracks I followed led to an old tree house deep in the woods," Velma replied. "What did you find?" she asked Fred and Daphne.

"We checked out the statue of the Lone Wolf," Fred said. "It really was smashed like Flint said."

"But we also found something else," Daphne added. "We looked in the bushes around the statue and found this."

Fred showed everyone a big steel hammer.

"Hmm," Velma said, tapping her finger to her chin. "I seem to remember seeing a hammer like this somewhere else."

"Me too," Fred said. "It looks to me like this wolfman's howled at his last full moon."

"Fred's right," Velma agreed. "It's time to set a trap."

"No way, man," Shaggy said. "I'm not going to let any wolfman take me for another ride."

"Re reither," Scooby said.

Just then, Colt walked out of the

bunkhouse. Colt's right arm was in a sling. He saw the gang in the corral and walked over to them.

"How's your arm, Colt?" Fred asked.

"Just a little sprain," Colt said. "Nothing to worry about."

Velma looked around. "Where's Flint?" she asked.

"He's searching the woods," Colt said. "He's convinced that Cal's behind all this. How's your detective work going?"

"We're about to set a trap to catch the wolfman," Fred answered. "And I think we could use your help."

"I'll do anything you want," Colt said. "If word spreads about this wolfman, Flint and I will have to close the place down for sure." Colt looked sad at the thought of it.

"We were just trying to convince Shaggy and Scooby here to help us out," Daphne said. "And now I'm sure they'd love to pitch in, right, fellas?"

Scooby-Doo sat down and shook his head.

"Would you do it for a Scooby Snack?" Velma asked.

"Ruh-uh," Scooby said.

"How about for two Scooby Snacks?" Velma asked.

Scooby just turned his head away as if he didn't hear her.

"How about for two Scooby Snacks and one of Gabby's special peach cobblers?" Colt asked.

Scooby's eyes lit up. "Reach robbler? Oh roy, oh roy, oh roy!" His tail wagged and he jumped up and down.

"Scooby, you get to work on solving this mystery," Colt said. "I'll get Gabby started on that peach cobbler."

"And then gather everyone together," Fred said. "You're going to help us solve the mystery of the howling wolfman."

Chapter 7

*L*ater that day, the guests and workers at the ranch were gathered back in the corral. Gabby set up a barbecue lunch, and Colt was standing on the stage.

"Friends, you'll be happy to know that the box that was taken last night did not contain the real gold horseshoes," Colt said. "The box last night only had replicas in it. The real horseshoes are so valuable, we keep them buried in a secret place. So until we solve this mystery, we're going to keep the real gold horseshoes locked up in the bank's vault. I'll be getting them in just a little while to bring them to town. I hope you'll enjoy your lunch and have a good afternoon."

Colt carefully jumped off the stage and walked over to the gang.

"That was perfect, Colt," Velma said. "If my hunch is right, the wolfman will be watching you very closely."

"That will stop everyone from worrying," Daphne said. "Speaking of worrying, where's Scooby-Doo?"

Shaggy pointed to the lunch table. Scooby-Doo was building himself a great big barbecue sandwich. Shaggy tiptoed up behind Scooby. Just as Scooby was about to take a bite, Shaggy grabbed him.

"Aaaaaa-ooooooooooh!" Shaggy howled.

"Rikes!" Scooby yelped. He dropped the sandwich and dove under the table. Shaggy caught the sandwich before it could hit the ground.

"Thanks, Scoob, old pal," Shaggy said.

He smiled and took a great big bite. "That really hit the spot."

"Enough fooling around, you two," Fred said. "We need to get over to the barn to set the trap."

The gang walked out of the corral and over to the barn. It was dark inside. Four stalls lined each side. Horses stood inside some of the stalls. Bales of hay were stacked all around, and small mounds of loose hay and straw covered the floor.

"Here's the plan," Fred began. "Colt is going to come in here pretending to dig up the horseshoes."

"And the wolfman is sure to follow," Velma added. "When the wolfman comes in, Daphne and I will close the doors from the outside."

"When I give the signal," Fred said, "Colt will lasso the wolfman. Shaggy, Scooby, and I will jump out and keep him from running away. Okay?"

"No way!" Scooby said.

"Oh, I almost forgot," Velma said. "I still owe you two Scooby Snacks."

"And reach robbler," Scooby said. His big pink tongue licked his lips.

"That you'll get *after* we catch the wolfman," Daphne said.

"But the Scooby Snacks you can have now," Velma said. She took two snacks out of her pocket and tossed them into the air one at a time. Scooby jumped up and caught the first one. Scooby jumped up for the second one. But before he could get it, a horse stretched out his head and gulped it down.

"Ruh?" Scooby said.

Fred looked at his watch. "It's almost time," he said. "Daphne, Velma, you two go outside and wait. I'll be over there behind those bales of hay. Shaggy, Scooby, you two hide in one of the stalls. And remember, don't make a sound."

"Like, no problem, Fredaroony," Shaggy said. "You can count on us."

Chapter 8

Shaggy and Scooby crept into one of the empty horse stalls. They sat down on a big pile of hay.

"Ree-hee-hee," Scooby giggled as he jumped up.

"What is it, Scoob?" Shaggy asked.

"Rickles," Scooby barked as he scratched himself all over.

"Like, the hay is tickling me, too," Shaggy said.

"Would you two knock it off?" Fred called. "They'll be here any minute."

Shaggy reached up and pulled Scooby-

Doo back down. A moment later, they heard the barn door creak open and close.

"That must be Colt," Shaggy whispered to Scooby.

They heard some footsteps pass by the stall. A moment later, the barn door creaked open again. Scooby slowly peeked over the edge of the stall.

He saw the wolfman slowly walking into the barn. Shaggy reached up and pulled Scooby down again. This time Scooby's face landed in a small pile of hay.

The wolfman's heavy paws dragged through the hay on the barn floor. Shaggy turned to say something to Scooby. He saw Scooby's nose starting to twitch.

"Like, hold on, Scoob," Shaggy pleaded. "This is no time for a Scooby sneeze."

The wolfman stopped in the middle of the barn. He turned around as if he heard something. Fred and Colt quietly stood up.

Colt grabbed his lasso and raised his arm to throw the rope.

"Raaaaaaaa-chooooooooooooooo!" sneezed Scooby.

Colt dropped his lasso. The wolfman spun around. The horses got scared. They whinnied and jumped around in their stalls.

"Get him before he gets away!" Colt yelled. The wolfman ran toward the barn door. On the way, he opened all of the horses' stalls. Fred and Colt started after the wolfman. Colt ran so fast his hat flew off his

head. It landed right on Scooby-Doo.

The hat covered Scooby's eyes. As he ran, he bumped into one of the horses. His paw got caught on the saddle. Before he knew it, Scooby was thrown onto the horse and was riding it out of the barn.

"Scooby-Dooby-Doo!" Scooby barked.

"Ride 'em, Scooby!" Shaggy called. "Now get that wolfman!"

The wolfman ran across the corral toward the woods. As the horse followed the wolfman, Scooby bounced up and down on

the saddle. The wolfman made a sharp turn to the right. The horse made a sharp turn to the right. The wolfman ran toward the bunkhouse. The horse ran toward the bunkhouse. The wolfman made a quick turn to the left. The horse made a quick turn to the left. The wolfman ran straight for the woods. The horse ran straight for the woods. The horse suddenly stopped, but Scooby kept going.

"Relp! Raggy!" Scooby barked. He flew through the air and landed right on top of the wolfman!

Chapter 9

Everyone ran over to Scooby and the wolfman.

"Way to go, Scooby," Shaggy said. He helped Scooby up. Colt and Fred lifted up the wolfman and held him tightly.

"Now, let's see who the wolfman really is," Fred said.

"Hold on a minute!" someone yelled from the woods. It was Flint Hopster. He was walking with Coyote Cal. Coyote Cal carried the metal box under his arm. As soon as they arrived, Colt reached over and lifted off the wolfman's furry mask.

"Bucky Tanner!" Colt and Flint exclaimed together.

"That's right," Fred said.

"But why?" Colt asked.

"Why don't you ask the brains behind it?" Velma said. She and Daphne escorted Gabby Tanner over to the crowd.

"I'm not ashamed of anything," Gabby said. "I had Bucky steal the horseshoes so we could buy the ranch ourselves and start a chain of Wild West restaurants. We would have been rich."

"But how did you know it was Gabby and Bucky?" Colt asked the gang.

"We didn't at first," Fred replied. "Flint was our first suspect."

"But we knew he would never do anything to hurt his twin brother," Daphne said. "No matter how much he disagreed with him."

"Then Coyote Cal became our main suspect," Velma said. "After all, he had been warning everyone about the wolfman for days."

"And he didn't make any secret about wanting to run the ranch by himself," Fred added.

"But what about the other clues you found?" Colt asked. "Like the denim cloth and the hammer by the broken statue."

"They were left out to make us think Coyote Cal was the wolfman," Velma said. "Take a closer look at the hammer."

Velma handed Colt the hammer they had found by the smashed statue. He and Flint looked at it carefully.

"This isn't a horseshoe hammer," Flint said.

"That's right," Daphne said. "It's a meat tenderizer. Like the one a cook would use to prepare meat for a big barbecue."

"But the clue that

really tipped us off," Velma said, "was the tree house I found when I followed the wolf-man's footprints."

"I followed the tracks there, too," Cal said. "That's where I found the box with the fake horseshoes."

"Before today, only two people ever knew about that old tree house: me and Bucky Tanner," Fred said. "And that's because we're the ones who built it as a secret hideout when we were kids."

Flint turned to Coyote Cal. "I'm sorry for thinking you were behind all this, Cal," Flint said.

"And thanks for recovering the horse-shoes," Colt added.

Then Colt and Flint turned and looked at Gabby.

"What do you have to say for yourself, Gabby?" Colt asked.

"Only that I would have gotten away with everything," Gabby said, "if it wasn't for those kids and their meddling mutt."

Coyote Cal grabbed Bucky by the scruff of his wolf costume and led him away. Flint followed with Gabby.

"Thanks so much for your help," Colt said. "You did more than save the ranch. You helped Flint and me realize that family is more important than any piece of land. We're going to work out something to save the ranch that will make both of us happy."

The next day, the gang piled into the

Mystery Machine to leave. On the drive out of the ranch, Shaggy looked out the window.

"Hey, look at that!" Shaggy said. Fred stopped the van. Coyote Cal was carving a new statue to guard the ranch. But instead of the gray wolf, it was a big wooden statue of Scooby-Doo.

"Scooby-Dooby-Dooooooooooooooooooo!" Scooby howled.

Cal waved and everyone laughed as the Mystery Machine continued on its way.

About the Author

As a boy, James Gelsey used to run home from school to watch the Scooby-Doo cartoons on television (only after finishing his homework). Today, he still enjoys watching them with his wife and daughter. He also has a real dog named Scooby who loves nothing more than a good Scooby Snack!

Solve a Mystery With Scooby-Doo!

SCOOBY-DOO! MYSTERIES

by James Gelsey

Ruh-roh!

Zoinks!

2 1982 03023 7303

APR   2013